## CASSIE'S FRIENDS

Each day when Cassie opened her window, the trees whispered down a song of morning greeting. The giant old pines and hickories, beeches and walnuts in the forest surrounding the house had stood there for centuries, strong and sheltering.

"Good morning, Mr. Trees," Cassie shouted. They would answer her with a soft, swooshing sound. "Hear 'em, Stacey?" Cassie would ask her brother. "Hear 'em singing?"

"Ah, cut that out, Cassie. Them trees ain't singing. How many times I gotta tell you that's just the wind?"

## SONG OF THE TREES
### *Mildred D. Taylor*

"A moving story that manifests two simple, strongly felt emotions: a love of nature and a sense of self-respect. . . . The writing style . . . backs up the element of dignity in the story's message and in its well-drawn black characters."

—*Booklist*

"A moving story of love, courage and personal integrity . . . a fine example of the literary excellence now becoming available."

—*St. Louis Post-Dispatch*

# Song of the Trees

by Mildred D. Taylor

Illustrated by Jerry Pinkney

LAUREL-LEAF BOOKS

*Published by*
*Bantam Doubleday Dell Books for Young Readers*
*a division of*
*Bantam Doubleday Dell Publishing Group, Inc.*
*1540 Broadway*
*New York, New York 10036*

*The trademark Laurel-Leaf Library® is registered in the U.S. Patent and Trademark Office.*
*The trademark Dell® is registered in the U.S. Patent and Trademark Office.*

*ISBN: 0-440-22699-6*

*RL: 6.0*

*Reprinted by arrangement with Dial Books for Young Readers*

*Printed in the United States of America*

*August 1996*

10  9  8  7  6

*This book is dedicated:*

*To my mother, Mrs. Deletha M. Taylor, the quiet, lovely one, who urged perseverance;*

*To my father, Mr. Wilbert L. Taylor, the strong, steadfast one, who wove the tales of history;*

*To my sister, Miss Wilma M. Taylor, the beautiful, laughing one, who lifted my spirits high;*

*and*

*To my grandparents, Mrs. Lee Annie Bryant, Mr. Hugh Taylor, and Mrs. Lou Emma Taylor, the wise ones, who bridged the generations between slavery and freedom;*

*and*

*To the Family, who fought and survived.*

This book is based on a true story, one that actually happened in my family. As a small child, I often listened to my father recount his adventures growing up in rural Mississippi during the Depression. His vivid description of the giant trees, the coming of the lumbermen, and the events that followed made me feel that I too was present. I hope my readers will be as moved by the story as I was.

*Mildred D. Taylor*
October 1974

# Song of the Trees

"Cassie. Cassie, child, wake up now," Big Ma called gently as the new sun peeked over the horizon.

I looked sleepily at my grandmother and closed my eyes again.

"Cassie! Get up, girl!" This time the voice was not so gentle.

I jumped out of the deep feathery bed a
Big Ma climbed from the other side. The
room was still dark, and I stubbed my toe
while stumbling sleepily about looking fo
my clothes.

"Shoot! Darn ole chair," I fussed, rubbing
my injured foot.

"Hush, Cassie, and open them curtains i
you can't see," Big Ma said. "Prop that win
dow open, too, and let some of that fresh
morning air in here."

I opened the window and looked outside
The earth was draped in a cloak of gray mist
as the sun chased the night away. The cotton
stalks, which in another hour would glisten
greenly toward the sun, were gray. The ri
pening corn, wrapped in jackets of emerald
and gold, was gray. Even the rich brown
Mississippi earth was gray.

Only the trees of the forest were not gray
They stood dark, almost black, across the
dusty road, still holding the night. A sof
breeze stirred, and their voices whispered
down to me in a song of morning greeting.

"Cassie, girl, I said open that window, no
stand there gazing out all morning. Now, ge

moving before I take something to you," Big
Ma threatened.

I dashed to my clothes. Before Big Ma had
unwoven her long braid of gray hair, my
pants and shirt were on and I was hurrying
into the kitchen.

A small kerosine lamp was burning in a
corner as I entered. Its light reflected on
seven-year-old Christopher-John, short,
pudgy, and a year younger than me, sitting
sleepily upon a side bench drinking a large
glass of clabber milk. Mama's back was to
me. She was dipping flour from a near-
empty canister, while my older brother,
Stacey, built a fire in the huge iron-bellied
stove.

"I don't know what I'm going to do with
you, Christopher-John," Mama scolded.
"Getting up in the middle of the night and
eating all that cornbread. Didn't you have
enough to eat before you went to bed?"

"Yes'm," Christopher-John murmured.

"Lord knows I don't want any of my
babies going hungry, but times are hard,
honey. Don't you know folks all around here
in Mississippi are struggling? Children crying cause they got no food to eat, and their

daddies crying cause they can't get jobs so they can feed their babies? And you getting up in the middle of the night, stuffing yourself with cornbread!"

Her voice softened as she looked at the sleepy little boy. "Baby, we're in a depression. Why do you think Papa's way down in Louisiana laying tracks on the railroad? So his children can eat—but only when they're hungry. You understand?"

"Yes'm," Christopher-John murmured again as his eyes slid blissfully shut.

"Morning, Mama," I chimed.

"Morning, baby," Mama said. "You wash up yet?"

"No'm."

"Then go wash up and call Little Man again. Tell him he's not dressing to meet President Roosevelt this morning. Hurry up now cause I want you to set the table."

Little Man, a very small six-year-old and a most finicky dresser, was brushing his hair when I entered the room he shared with Stacey and Christopher-John. His blue pants were faded, but except for a small grass stain on one knee, they were clean. Outside of his Sunday pants, these were the

only pants he had, and he was always careful to keep them in the best condition possible. But one look at him and I knew that he was far from pleased with their condition this morning. He frowned down at the spot for a moment, then continued brushing.

"Man, hurry up and get dressed," I called. "Mama said you ain't dressing to meet the president."

"See there," he said, pointing at the stain. "You did that."

"I did no such thing. You fell all by yourself."

"You tripped me!"

"Didn't!"

"Did, too!"

"Hey, cut it out, you two!" ordered Stacey, entering the room. "You fought over that stupid stain yesterday. Now get moving, both of you. We gotta go pick blackberries before the sun gets too high. Little Man, you go gather the eggs while Christopher-John and me milk the cows."

Little Man and I decided to settle our dispute later when Stacey wasn't around. With Papa away, eleven-year-old Stacey thought of himself as the man of the house, and Mama had instructed Little Man, Christopher-John, and me to mind him. So, like it or not, we humored him. Besides, he was bigger than we were.

I ran to the back porch to wash. When I returned to the kitchen, Mama was talking to Big Ma.

"We got about enough flour for two more meals," Mama said, cutting the biscuit dough. "Our salt and sugar are practically down to nothing and ——" She stopped when she saw me. "Cassie, baby, go gather the eggs for Mama."

"Little Man's gathering the eggs."

"Then go help him."

"But I ain't set the table yet."

"Set it when you come back."

I knew that I was not wanted in the kitchen. I looked suspiciously at my mother and grandmother, then went to the back porch to get a basket.

Big Ma's voice drifted through the open window. "Mary, you oughta write David and tell him somebody done opened his letter and stole that ten dollars he sent," she said.

"No, Mama. David's got enough on his

nind. Besides, there's enough garden foods
o we won't go hungry."

"But what 'bout your medicine? You're
ıll out of it and the doctor told you good to
—''

"Shhhh!" Mama stared at the window.
'Cassie, I thought I told you to go gather
hose eggs!"

"I had to get a basket, Mama!" I hurried
off the porch and ran to the barn.

After breakfast when the sun was streak-
ng red across the sky, my brothers and I
ambled into the coolness of the forest lead-
ng our three cows and their calves down
he narrow cow path to the pond. The morn-
ng was already muggy, but the trees closed
out the heat as their leaves waved restlessly,
high above our heads.

"Good morning, Mr. Trees," I shouted.
They answered me with a soft, swooshing
sound. "Hear 'em, Stacey? Hear 'em sing-
ng?"

"Ah, cut that out, Cassie. Them trees ain't
singing. How many times I gotta tell you
hat's just the wind?" He stopped at a sweet
alligator gum, pulled out his knife and
scraped off a glob of gum that had seeped

through its cracked bark. He handed me half.

As I stuffed the gooey wad into my mouth, I patted the tree and whispered, "Thank you, Mr. Gum Tree."

Stacey frowned at me, then looked back at Christopher-John and Little Man walking far behind us, munching on their breakfast biscuits.

"Man! Christopher-John! Come on, now," he yelled. "If we finish the berry picking early, we can go wading before we go back."

Christopher-John and Little Man ran to catch up with us. Then, resuming their leisurely pace, they soon fell behind again.

A large gray squirrel scurried across our path and up a walnut tree. I watched until it was settled amidst the tree's featherlike leaves; then, poking one of the calves, I said, "Stacey, is Mama sick?"

"Sick? Why you say that?"

"Cause I heard Big Ma asking her 'bout some medicine she's supposed to have."

Stacey stopped, a worried look on his face. "If she's sick, she ain't bad sick," he

decided. "If she was bad sick, she'd been in bed."

We left the cows at the pond and, taking our berry baskets, delved deeper into the forest looking for the wild blackberry bushes.

"I see one!" I shouted.

"Where?" cried Christopher-John, eager for the sweet berries.

"Over there! Last one to it's a rotten egg!" I yelled, and off I ran.

Stacey and Little Man followed at my heels. But Christopher-John puffed far behind. "Hey, wait for me," he cried.

"Let's hide from Christopher-John," Stacey suggested.

The three of us ran in different directions. I plunged behind a giant old pine and hugged its warm trunk as I waited for Christopher-John.

Christopher-John puffed to a stop; then, looking all around, called, "Hey, Stacey! Cassie! Hey, Man! Y'all cut that out!"

I giggled and Christopher-John heard me.

"I see you, Cassie!" he shouted, starting toward me as fast as his chubby legs would carry him. "You're it!"

"Not 'til you tag me," I laughed. As I waited for him to get closer, I glanced up into the boughs of my wintry-smelling hiding tree expecting a song of laughter. But the old pine only tapped me gently with one of its long, low branches. I turned from the tree and dashed away.

"You can't, you can't, you can't catch me," I taunted, dodging from one beloved tree to the next. Around shaggy-bark hickories and sharp-needled pines, past blue-gray beeches and sturdy black walnuts I sailed while my laughter resounded through the ancient forest, filling every chink. Overhead, the boughs of the giant trees hovered protectively, but they did not join in my laughter.

Deeper into the forest I plunged.

Christopher-John, unable to keep up, plopped on the ground in a pant. Little Man and Stacey, emerging from their hiding places, ran up to him.

"Ain't you caught her yet?" Little Man demanded, more than a little annoyed.

"He can't catch the champ," I boasted, stopping to rest against a hickory tree. I slid my back down the tree's shaggy trunk and

ooked up at its long branches, heavy with sweet nuts and slender green leaves, perfectly still. I looked around at the leaves of the other trees. They were still also. I stared at the trees, aware of an eerie silence descending over the forest.

Stacey walked toward me. "What's the matter with you, Cassie?" he asked.

"The trees, Stacey," I said softly, "they ain't singing no more."

"Is that all?" He looked up at the sky. "Come on, y'all. It's getting late. We'd better go pick them berries." He turned and walked on.

"But, Stacey, listen. Little Man, Christopher-John, listen."

The forest echoed an uneasy silence.

"The wind just stopped blowing, that's all," said Stacey. "Now stop fooling around and come on."

I jumped up to follow Stacey, then cried, "Stacey, look!" On a black oak a few yards away was a huge white X. "How did that get here?" I exclaimed, running to the tree.

"There's another one!" Little Man screamed.

"I see one too!" shouted Christopher-John.

Stacey said nothing as Christopher-John, Little Man and I ran wildly through the forest counting the ghostlike marks.

"Stacey, they're on practically all of them," I said when he called us back. Why?"

Stacey studied the trees, then suddenly pushed us down.

"My clothes!" Little Man wailed indignantly.

"Hush, Man, and stay down," Stacey warned. "Somebody's coming."

Two white men emerged. We looked at each other. We knew to be silent.

"You mark them all down here?" one of the men asked.

"Not the younger ones, Mr. Andersen."

"We might need them, too," said Mr. Andersen, counting the X's. "But don't worry 'bout marking them now, Tom. We'll get them later. Also them trees up past the pond toward the house."

"The old woman agree to you cutting these trees?"

"I ain't been down there yet," Mr. Andersen said.

"Mr. Andersen . . ." Tom hesitated a moment, looked up at the silent trees, then back at Mr. Andersen. "Maybe you should go easy with them," he cautioned. "You know that David can be as mean as an ole jackass when he wanna be."

"He's talking about Papa," I whispered.

"Shhhh!" Stacey hissed.

Mr. Andersen looked uneasy. "What's that gotta do with anything?"

"Well, he just don't take much to any dealings with white folks." Again, Tom looked up at the trees. "He ain't afraid like some."

Mr. Andersen laughed weakly. "Don't worry 'bout that, Tom. The land belongs to his mama. He don't have no say in it. Besides, I guess I oughta know how to handle David Logan. After all, there are ways. . . .

"Now, you get on back to my place and get some boys and start chopping down these trees," Mr. Andersen said. "I'll go talk to the old woman." He looked up at the sky. "We can almost get a full day's work in if we hurry."

Mr. Andersen turned to walk away, but Tom stopped him. "Mr. Andersen, you really gonna chop all the trees?"

"If I need to. These folks ain't got no call for them. I do. I got me a good contract for these trees and I aim to fulfill it."

Tom watched Mr. Andersen walk away; then, looking sorrowfully up at the trees, he shook his head and disappeared into the depths of the forest.

"What we gonna do, Stacey?" I asked anxiously. "They can't just cut down our trees, can they?"

"I don't know. Papa's gone . . ." Stacey muttered to himself, trying to decide what we should do next.

"Boy, if Papa was here, them ole white men wouldn't be messing with our trees," Little Man declared.

"Yeah!" Christopher-John agreed. "Just let Papa get hold of 'em and he gonna turn 'em every which way but loose."

"Christopher-John, Man," Stacey said finally, "go get the cows and take them home."

"But we just brought them down here," Little Man protested.

"And we gotta pick the berries for dinner," said Christopher-John mournfully.

"No time for that now. Hurry up. And stay

clear of them white men. Cassie, you come with me."

We ran, brown legs and feet flying high through the still forest.

By the time Stacey and I arrived at the house, Mr. Andersen's car was already parked in the dusty drive. Mr. Andersen himself was seated comfortably in Papa's rocker on the front porch. Big Ma was seated too, but Mama was standing.

Stacey and I eased quietly to the side of the porch, unnoticed.

"Sixty-five dollars. That's an awful lot of money in these hard times, Aunt Caroline," Mr. Andersen was saying to Big Ma.

I could see Mama's thin face harden.

"You know," Mr. Andersen said, rocking familiarly in Papa's chair, "that's more than David can send home in two months."

"We do quite well on what David sends home," Mama said coldly.

Mr. Andersen stopped rocking. "I suggest you encourage Aunt Caroline to sell them trees, Mary. You know, David might not always be able to work so good. He could possibly have . . . an accident."

Big Ma's soft brown eyes clouded over

with fear as she looked first at Mr. Anderse
then at Mama. But Mama clenched her fis
and said, "In Mississippi, black men do n
have accidents."

"Hush, child, hush," Big Ma said hu
riedly. "How many trees for the sixty-fi\
dollars, Mr. Andersen?"

"Enough 'til I figure I got my sixty-fi\
dollars' worth."

"And how many would that be?" Man
persisted.

Mr. Andersen looked haughtily at Mam
"I said I'd be the judge of that, Mary."

"I think not," Mama said.

Mr. Andersen stared at Mama. And Man
stared back at him. I knew Mr. Anderse
didn't like that, but Mama did it anywa
Mr. Andersen soon grew uneasy under th
piercing gaze, and when his eyes swift
shifted from Mama to Big Ma, his face w:
beet-red.

"Caroline," he said, his voice low an
menacing, "you're the head of this fami
and you've got a decision to make. Now,
need them trees and I mean to have ther
I've offered you a good price for them and

ain't gonna haggle over it. I know y'all can use the money. Doc Thomas tells me that Mary's not well." He hesitated a moment, then hissed venomously, "And if something should happen to David . . ."

"All right," Big Ma said, her voice trembling. "All right, Mr. Andersen."

"No, Big Ma!" I cried, leaping onto the porch. "You can't let him cut our trees!"

Mr. Andersen grasped the arms of the rocker, his knuckles chalk white. "You certainly ain't taught none of your younguns how to behave, Caroline," he said curtly.

"You children go on to the back," Mama said, shooing us away.

"No, Mama," Stacey said. "He's gonna cut them all down. Me and Cassie heard him say so in the woods."

"I won't let him cut them," I threatened. "I won't let him! The trees are my friends and ain't no mean ole white man gonna touch my trees——"

Mama's hands went roughly around my body as she carried me off to my room.

"Now, hush," she said, her dark eyes flashing wildly. "I've told you how dangerous it is . . ." She broke off in midsentence. She stared at me a moment, then hugged me tightly and went back to the porch.

Stacey joined me a few seconds later, and we sat there in the heat of the quiet room, listening miserably as the first whack of an ax echoed against the trees.

That night I was awakened by soft sounds outside my window. I reached for Big Ma, but she wasn't there. Hurrying to the window, I saw Mama and Big Ma standing in the yard in their night clothes and Stacey, fully dressed, sitting atop Lady, our golden mare. By the time I got outside, Stacey was gone.

"Mama, where's Stacey?" I cried.

"Be quiet, Cassie. You'll wake Christopher-John and Little Man."

"But where's he going?"

"He's going to get Papa," Mama said. "Now be quiet."

"Go on Stacey, boy," I whispered. "Ride for me, too."

As the dust billowed after him, Mama said, "I should've gone myself. He's so young."

Big Ma put her arm around Mama. "Now, Mary, you know you couldn't 've gone. Mr. Andersen would miss you if he come by and see you ain't here. You done right, now. Don't worry, that boy'll be just fine."

Three days passed, hot and windless. Mama forbade any of us to go into the forest, so Christopher-John, Little Man and I spent the slow, restless days hovering as close to the dusty road as we dared, listening to the foreign sounds of steel against the trees and the thunderous roar of those ancient loved ones as they crashed upon the earth. Sometimes Mama would scold us and tell us to come back to the house, but even she could not ignore the continuous pounding of the axes against the trees. Or the sight of the loaded lumber wagons rolling out of the forest. In the middle of washing or ironing or hoeing, she would look up sorrowfully and listen, then turn toward the road, searching for some sign of Papa and Stacey.

On the fourth day, before the sun had risen bringing its cloak of miserable heat, I saw her walking alone toward the woods. I ran after her.

She did not send me back.

"Mama," I said, "How sick are you?"

Mama took my hand. "Remember whe you had the flu and felt so sick?"

"Yes'm."

"And when I gave you some medicine you got well soon afterward?"

"Yes'm."

"Well, that's how sick I am. As soon as get my medicine, I'll be all well again. An that'll be soon now that Papa's comin home," she said, giving my hand a gentl little squeeze.

The quiet surrounded us as we entere the forest. Mama clicked on the flashligl and we walked silently along the cow pat to the pond. There, just beyond the pon pockets of open space loomed before us.

"Mama!"

"I know, baby, I know."

On the ground lay countless trees. Tree that had once been such strong, tall thing So strong that I could fling my arms partiall around one of them and feel safe and secur So tall and leafy green that their boughs ha formed a forest temple.

And old.

So old that Indians had once built fires at
their feet and had sung happy songs of
happy days. So old, they had hidden fleeing
black men in the night and listened to their
old tales of a foreign land.

In the cold of winter when the ground lay
frozen, they had sung their frosty ballads of
years gone by. Or on a muggy, sweat-
drenched day, their leaves had rippled
softly, lazily, like restless green fingers
strumming at a guitar, echoing their epic
tales.

But now they would sing no more. They
lay forever silent upon the ground.

Those trees that remained standing were
like defeated warriors mourning their fallen
dead. But soon they, too, would fall, for the
white X's had been placed on nearly every
one.

"Oh, dear, dear trees," I cried as the gray
light of the rising sun fell in ghostly
shadows over the land. The tears rolled hot
down my cheeks. Mama held me close, and
when I felt her body tremble, I knew she
was crying too.

When our tears eased, we turned sadly toward the house. As we emerged from the forest, we could see two small figures waiting impatiently on the other side of the road. As soon as they spied us, they hurried across to meet us.

"Mama! You and Cassie was in the forest," Little Man accused. "Big Ma told us!"

"How was it?" asked Christopher-John, rubbing the sleep from his eyes. "Was it spooky?"

"Spooky and empty," I said listlessly.

"Mama, me and Christopher-John wanna see too," Little Man declared.

"No, baby," Mama said softly as we crossed the road. "The men'll be down there soon, and I don't want y'all underfoot."

"But, Mama——" Little Man started to protest.

"When Papa comes home and the men are gone, then you can go. But until then, you stay out of there. You hear me, Little Man Logan?"

"Yes'm," Little Man reluctantly replied.

But the sun had been up only an hour

when Little Man decided that he could not wait for Papa to return.

"Mama said we wasn't to go down there," Christopher-John warned.

"Cassie did," Little Man cried.

"But she was with Mama. Wasn't you, Cassie?"

"Well, I'm going too," said Little Man. "Everybody's always going someplace 'cepting me." And off he went.

Christopher-John and I ran after him. Down the narrow cow path and around the pond we chased. But neither of us was fast enough to overtake Little Man before he reached the lumbermen.

"Hey, you kids, get away from here," Mr. Andersen shouted when he saw us. "Now, y'all go on back home," he said, stopping in front of Little Man.

"We are home," I said. "You're the one who's on our land."

"Claude," Mr. Andersen said to one of the black lumbermen, "take these kids home." Then he pushed Little Man out of his way. Little Man pushed back. Mr. Andersen looked down, startled that a little black boy would do such a thing. He shoved Little

Man a second time, and Little Man fell int
the dirt.

Little Man looked down at his clothin
covered with sawdust and dirt, and wailec
"You got my clothes dirty!"

I rushed toward Mr. Andersen, my fist in
mighty hammer, shouting, "You ain't got n
right to push on Little Man. Why don't yo
push on somebody your own size—like me
you ole——"

The man called Claude put his hand ove
my mouth and carried me away. Chris
topher-John trailed behind us, tugging o
the man's shirt.

"Put her down. Hey, mister, put Cassi
down."

The man carried me all the way to th
pond. "Now," he said, "you and you
brothers get on home before y'all get hur
Go on, get!"

As the man walked away, I looked arounc
"Where's Little Man?"

Christopher-John looked around too.

"I don't know," he said. "I thought he wa
behind me."

Back we ran toward the lumbermen.

We found Little Man's clothing firs

folded neatly by a tree. Then we saw Little Man, dragging a huge stick, and headed straight for Mr. Andersen.

"Little Man, come back here," I called.

But Little Man did not stop.

Mr. Andersen stood alone, barking orders, unaware of the oncoming Little Man.

"Little Man! Oh, Little Man, don't!"

It was too late.

Little Man swung the stick as hard as he could against Mr. Andersen's leg.

Mr. Andersen let out a howl and reached to where he thought Little Man's collar was. But, of course, Little Man had no collar.

"Run, Man!" Christopher-John and I shouted. "Run!"

"Why, you little . . ." Mr. Andersen cried, grabbing at Little Man. But Little Man was too quick for him. He slid right through Mr. Andersen's legs. Tom stood nearby, his face crinkling into an amused grin.

"Hey, y'all!" Mr. Andersen yelled to the lumbermen. "Claude! Get that kid!"

But sure-footed Little Man dodged the groping hands of the lumbermen as easily as if he were skirting mud puddles. Over tree stumps, around legs and through legs he dashed. But in the end, there were too many lumbermen for him, and he was handed over to Mr. Andersen.

For the second time, Christopher-John and I went to Little Man's rescue.

"Put him down!" we ordered, charging the lumbermen.

I was captured much too quickly, though not before I had landed several stinging blows. But Christopher-John, furious at seeing Little Man handled so roughly by Mr. Andersen, managed to elude the clutches of the lumbermen until he was fully upon Mr. Andersen. Then, with his mightiest thrust, he kicked Mr. Andersen solidly in the shins, not once, but twice, before the lumbermen pulled him away.

Mr. Andersen was fuming. He slowly took off his wide leather belt. Christopher-John, Little Man and I looked woefully at the belt, then at each other. Little Man and Christopher-John fought to escape, but I closed my eyes and awaited the whining of the heavy belt and its painful bite against my skin.

What was he waiting for? I started to open my eyes, but then the zinging whirl of the belt began and I tensed, awaiting its fearful sting. But just as the leather tip lashed into my leg, a deep familiar voice said, "Put the belt down, Andersen."

I opened my eyes.

"Papa!"

"Let the children go," Papa said. He was standing on a nearby ridge with a strange black box in his hands. Stacey was behind him holding the reins to Lady.

The chopping stopped as all eyes turned to Papa.

"They been right meddlesome," Mr. Andersen said. "They need teaching how to act."

"Any teaching, I'll do it. Now, let them go."

Mr. Andersen looked down at Little Man struggling to get away. Smiling broadly, he motioned our release. "Okay, David," he said.

As we ran up the ridge to Papa, Mr. Andersen said, "It's good to have you home, boy."

Papa said nothing until we were safely behind him. "Take them home, Stacey."

"But, Papa——"

"Do like I say, son."

Stacey herded us away from the men.
When we were far enough away so Papa
couldn't see us, Stacey stopped and handed
me Lady's reins.

"Y'all go on home now," he said. "I gotta
go help Papa."

"Papa don't need no help," I said. "He
told you to come with us."

"But you don't know what he's gonna do."

"What?" I asked.

"He's gonna blow up the forest if they
don't get out of here. So go on home where
y'all be safe."

"How's he gonna do that?" asked Little
Man.

"We been setting sticks of dynamite since
the middle of the night. We ain't even been
up to the house cause Papa wanted the
sticks planted and covered over before the
men came. Now, Cassie, take them on back
to the house. Do like I tell you for once, will
ya?" Then, without waiting for another
word, he was gone.

"I wanna see," Little Man announced.

"I don't," protested Christopher-John.

"Come on," I said.

We tied the mare to a tree, then belly-crawled back to where we could see Papa and joined Stacey in the brush.

"Cassie, I told you . . ."

"What's Papa doing?"

The black box was now set upon a sawed-off tree stump, and Papa's hands were tightly grasping a T-shaped instrument which went into it.

"What's that thing?" asked Little Man.

"It's a plunger," Stacey whispered. "If Papa presses down on it, the whole forest will go pfffff!"

Our mouths went dry and our eyes went wide. Mr. Andersen's eyes were wide, too.

"You're bluffing, David," he said. "You ain't gonna push that plunger."

"One thing you can't seem to understand, Andersen," Papa said, "is that a black man's always gotta be ready to die. And it don't make me any difference if I die today or tomorrow. Just as long as I die right."

Mr. Andersen laughed uneasily. The lumbermen moved nervously away.

"I mean what I say," Papa said. "Ask any-one. I always mean what I say."

"He sure do, Mr. Andersen," Claude said eyeing the black box. "He always do."

"Shut up!" Mr. Andersen snapped. "And the rest of y'all stay put." Then turning back to Papa, he smiled cunningly. "I'm sure you and me can work something out David."

"Ain't nothing to be worked out," said Papa.

"Now, look here, David, your mama and me, we got us a contract . . ."

"There ain't no more contract," Papa replied coldly. "Now, either you get out or blow it up. That's it."

"He means it, Mr. Andersen," another frightened lumberman ventured. "He' crazy and he sure 'nough means it."

"You know what could happen to you boy?" Mr. Andersen exploded, his face beet-red again. "Threatening a white man like this?"

Papa said nothing. He just stood there, hi hands firmly on the plunger, staring down a Mr. Andersen.

Mr. Andersen could not bear the stare. He turned away, cursing Papa. "You're a fool David. A crazy fool." Then he looked

round at the lumbermen. They shifted
their eyes and would not look at him.

"Maybe we better leave, Mr. Andersen,"
Tom said quietly.

Mr. Andersen glanced at Tom, then
turned back to Papa and said as lightly as he
could, "All right, David, all right. It's your
land. We'll just take the logs we got cut and
get out." He motioned to the men. "Hey,
let's get moving and get these logs out of
here before this crazy fool gets us all killed."

"No," Papa said.

Mr. Andersen stopped, knowing that he
could not have heard correctly. "What you
say?"

"You ain't taking one more stick out of this
forest."

"Now, look here——"

"You heard me."

"But you can't sell all these logs, David,"
Mr. Andersen exclaimed incredulously.

Papa said nothing. Just cast that piercing
look on Mr. Andersen.

"Look, I'm a fair man. I tell you what I'll
do. I'll give you another thirty-five dollars.
An even hundred dollars. Now, that's fair,
ain't it?"

"I'll see them rot first."

"But——"

"That's my last word," Papa said, tighte
ing his grip on the plunger.

Mr. Andersen swallowed hard. "Y(
won't always have that black box, David
he warned. "You know that, don't you?"

"That may be. But it won't matter non
Cause I'll always have my self-respect."

Mr. Andersen opened his mouth to spea
but no sound came. Tom and the lumbe
men were quietly moving away, puttir
their gear in the empty lumber wagons. M
Andersen looked again at the black box. F
nally, his face ashen, he too walked away

Papa stood unmoving until the wagor
and the men were gone. Then, when th
sound of the last wagon rolling over the d
leaves could no longer be heard and a ho
low silence filled the air, he slowly remove
his hands from the plunger and looked up
the remaining trees standing like lone
sentries in the morning.

"Dear, dear old trees," I heard him ca
softly, "will you ever sing again?"

I waited. But the trees gave no answer

## ABOUT THE AUTHOR

MILDRED D. TAYLOR is the author of the 1977 Newbery Award-winning *Roll of Thunder, Hear My Cry* and its sequel, *Let the Circle Be Unbroken*.

Ms. Taylor was born in Jackson, Mississippi, and grew up in Toledo, Ohio. She was graduated from the University of Toledo and spent two years in Ethiopia with the Peace Corps. Returning to the United States, Ms. Taylor entered the University of Colorado's School of Journalism, from which she received her Master of Arts degree. As a member of the Black Student Alliance, she worked with students and university officials in structuring a Black Studies program at the university. She lives in Boulder, Colorado.

## ABOUT THE ILLUSTRATOR

JERRY PINKNEY grew up in Philadelphia and attended the Philadelphia Museum College of Art. He has been represented in the AIGA Best Books of the Year and the 100 Years of Illustration show at the Brooklyn Museum. He lives in Croton-on-Hudson, New York, with his wife, Gloria, and their four children.